Erika, you make both me and my books better
—Jens

Published in English in Canada and the USA in 2023 by Groundwood Books
in agreement with Koja Agency
Text copyright © 2018 by Jens Mattsson
Illustrations copyright © 2018 by Jenny Lucander
English translation copyright © 2023 by Brett Jocelyn Woodstein
First published in Swedish as *Vi är lajon!* copyright © 2018
by Natur & Kultur, Stockholm
The cost of this translation was defrayed by a subsidy from the Swedish Arts Council,
gratefully acknowledged.

Groundwood Books / House of Anansi Press
groundwoodbooks.com

We gratefully acknowledge the Government of Canada
for its financial support of our publishing program.

With the participation of the Government of Canada
Avec la participation du gouvernement du Canada | Canada

Library and Archives Canada Cataloguing in Publication
Title: We are lions! / words by Jens Mattsson ; pictures by Jenny Lucander ;
translated by B.J. Woodstein.
Other titles: Vi är lajon! English
Names: Mattsson, Jens, author | Lucander, Jenny, illustrator. | Epstein, B. J.,
translator.
Description: Translation of: Vi är lajon!
Identifiers: Canadiana (print) 20220268746 | Canadiana (ebook) 20220268754 | ISBN 9781773067018
(hardcover) | ISBN 9781773067025 (Kindle) | ISBN 9781773067032 (EPUB)
Classification: LCC PZ7.1.M38 W42 2023 | DDC j839.73/8—dc23

The illustrations were created with line drawings, watercolors and digital collage.

Printed and bound in South Korea

FSC
www.fsc.org
MIX
Paper | Supporting
responsible forestry
FSC® C140526

We Are LiONS!

Words by Jens Mattsson | Pictures by Jenny Lucander
Translated by B.J. Woodstein

GROUNDWOOD BOOKS   HOUSE OF ANANSI PRESS   TORONTO / BERKELEY

I am a lion. My big brother is one too. *ROOOOARR!*
We are a pride. We hunt gazelles and wildebeest on the savanna.
When we catch them, we eat them. We are dangerous!

When we hunt, we stalk silently. Mom Gazelle
and Dad Wildebeest don't notice a thing.
But sometimes we just laze in a lion heap.

One day, my brother doesn't want to run around the savanna. His stomach hurts.

I call him a poopy gazelle, but he doesn't even growl. He just whines. It's boring.

My brother has to go to the doctor. Dad doesn't listen when I say that lions go to the veterinarian. Mom wants us to sit and talk on the couch. Lions don't do that.

That night, my brother tells me that he got a shot.
And the doctor took some of his blood.

I do lion tricks to make him happy.
I growl and roar and claw. And pounce.

My brother has to see the doctor lots of times and take medicine. Then he even has to stay at the hospital, but I'm allowed to visit him. Mom says the medicine will make him better, but it will also make him lose his lion mane.

My brother's bed can go up and down,
and it has bars. Like a cage at a zoo.
But he isn't alone in it. Bronto, Bambi,
Blankie and Tufty are there too.
And the king of the forest, Mr. Moose.

Mom and Dad want me to sit with them and be calm.
They don't want me to fidget and fuss. But lions
have to hunt and make noise, even if Mom
and Dad and the doctor say no.
So I sneak into the bathroom and
roar and spill water on the floor.

My brother roars too, but weaker.
Roooaaar. Lions don't want to be
trapped by wires and tubes.

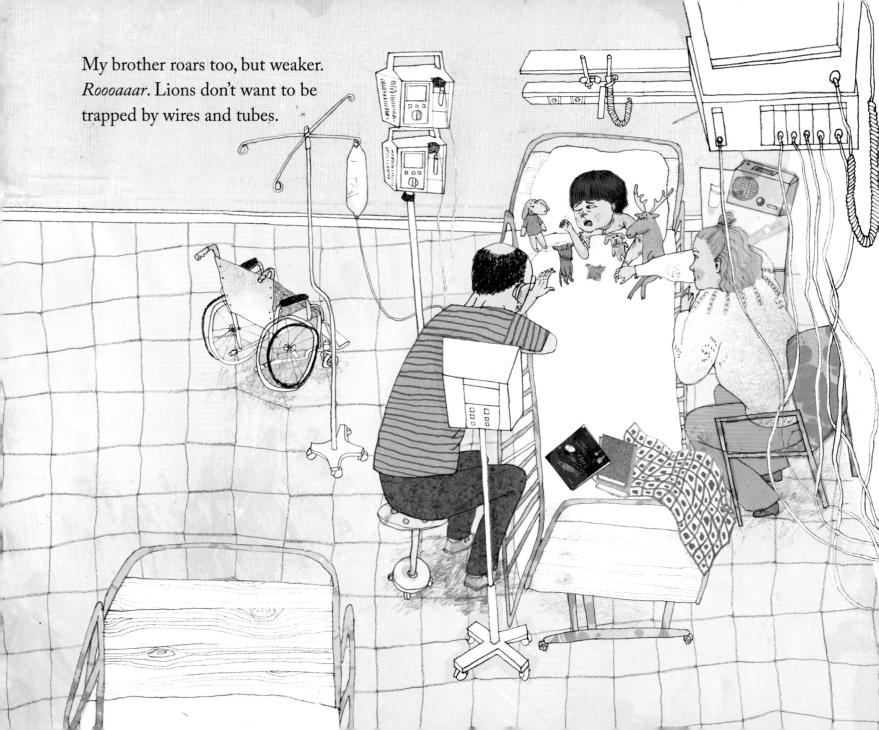

After Mom Gazelle leaves for work, we're super quiet
for a very long time. So long that Dad Wildebeest falls
asleep in his chair. I help my brother climb over the bars,
into a wheelchair and out into the hallway.

To the savanna! We're going to hunt
the old animals who can't get away and we're
going to eat them! That's what lions do.

By a watering hole, we find Old Lady Zebra with a walker.
But she just laughs when we show her our fangs.

Then we catch Old Man Hippo in pajamas, with a bandage on his head. He squeals when we lion-howl and rip him into pieces. Hippos are good for hunting because they really get scared.

Everyone comes running, but no one can stop lions on the hunt. Then my brother's IV gets caught on a door handle. The adventure is over. The pride is captured.

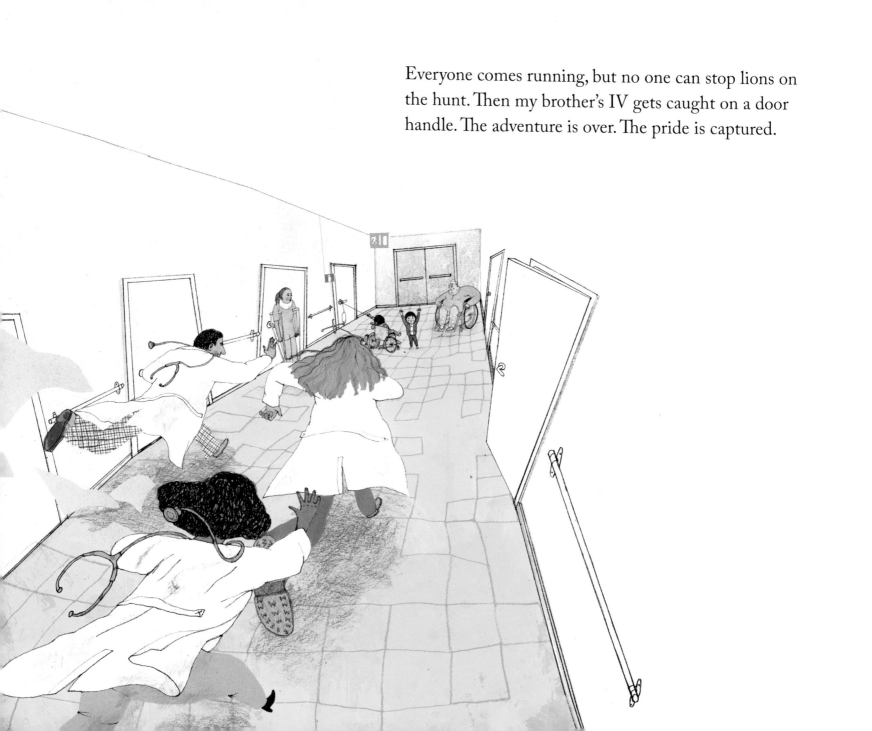

Dad sounds angry, but he hugs us tightly.
Naughty kids, he calls us. *Naughty lions*, I say.
My brother doesn't hear. He's already asleep.

My brother has almost no fur left. He looks like Grandpa.
But he has his own teeth, and he can still growl when someone
comes with medicine.

I tell him about preschool. No one there knows how to hunt.
They do it wrong. My brother understands exactly what I mean,
and I get to eat his whole dessert, even though it's chocolate
pudding. And I get to open the candy that Grandma and
Grandpa gave him.

It's cold outside, but warm inside. Mom shakes as if she's freezing.
Dad rearranges the flowers, even though they already look nice.

Lions can't cry. But they can feel small and alone. They can miss
the rest of their pride.

I get to climb over the bars and lie next to him. Mom and
Dad each hold a paw. I make claws with my fingers
against my brother's arm and growl.

We are lions, he whispers. I nod.

Soon we'll go hunting again.

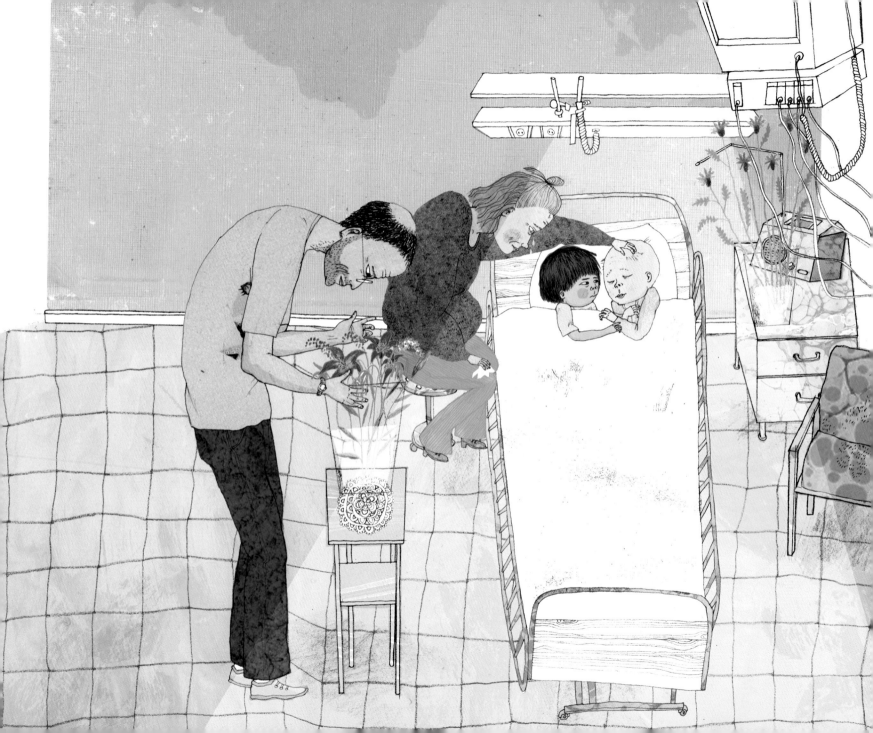